Sonnets of Ascent

LIZ AND TIM CARTER

ISBN 978-1-8382056-3-8

Published by Capstone House

Cover photo/design by Liz Carter

sonnet

noun

noun: **sonnet**; plural noun: **sonnets**

a poem of fourteen lines using any of a number of formal rhyme schemes, in English typically having ten syllables per line.

Contents

INTRODUCTION

I wonder if there's a book you've been meaning to read for a while. A classic that you've heard about, but never found the opportunity to get hold of, sit down, and read. (To be clear, I'm not suggesting that this is that book.) One of the many blessings of being an ordained minister in the Church of England is that every so often you are given the opportunity to have a Sabbatical, to take some time to reflect and refresh, and perhaps, read some of those books.

In the Spring of 2023 I had such an opportunity and one of the books on my list was *A Long Obedience in the Same Direction* by Eugene Peterson. I'd heard of it, had it recommended to me a number of times over the years, but knew very little about it, so I ordered it and added it to the pile. What I discovered was a deep and rich exploration of the practicalities of the life of Christian discipleship, structured around reflections on the Psalms of Ascent.

As I read these reflections, accompanied by the stripped back translations of the Psalms by Robert Alter, I felt a tingle of an idea. What would it look like to write poems inspired by these Psalms? What if I didn't do this on my own, but as a joint project with my wife, Liz?

So, as part of our Sabbatical, Liz and I set aside a couple of hours a day while we were on the Isle of Wight to read the Psalms together, to discuss our reflections on them, and to write a sonnet each, for each Psalm. We offer these to you with the prayer that they will inspire your creativity and engagement with the God who loves us, who speaks to us by Word and Spirit, and who calls us to ascend.

SONNETS OF ASCENT

PSALMS 120 ~ 134

Psalm 120 ~ Repentance

Lying lips and truthless tongues deceive,
Besetting ears, mis-shaping minds with claims
Flapping or focused. I'm caught in the weave.
Overflow of the heart, forest fire flames.

Heart aching for friendship, family, rest,
I wander among strangers, far from home.
Strange words, strange ways, strange wounds,
no place to nest.
Leaving me unsettled, unsure, unknown.

I seek peace and pursue it, truth on side,
to reconcile and restore peace while facts
are weaponised, falsehoods factified
in othering, warifying, hate speech acts.

Rescue me, save me, bring me home, I'm done
with this Lord God, you answer, "I'm your sun."

Psalm 120 ~ Repentance

Frailty taints my words, tumbling into pits
Never ending lies; overwhelming floods
Save me, oh my Lord, lighten lying lips
Sanctify my tongue; cleanse this mortal blood

God who dwells with us, holy-just you reign
You sigh at our hate, close your sacred eyes
Our shortfalls your grief; our conflict your pain
Your justice is true, you are God most High

Sick at anguished heart, longing for my home
This world is too far; I am not at ease
I will wait for you; heavy-hearted groans
I will lift my face; turn my sighs to peace

Sick at anguished heart, I am crying out
You are calling back; you call spirit-loud

PSALM 121 ~ PROVIDENCE

Lift up my eyes from the muddle of life
From mind diversions in temptation's ills
Dazzling beguilements that burn my heart rife
Lift up my eyes to superlative hills

Through wide open skies where pure
beauty streams
Majesty shivers through heaven's display
My helper, my maker: holy extremes
Your artistry splashed across each new day

You guard me on all my borders of haste
Your heed is freedom; your vigil my light
Your watchful unrest is my spacious place
Keep me soul-safe in your arms through the night

Arch me in safety; shelter my story
Forevermore, immerse me in glory

Psalm 121 ~ Providence

Ahead mountain paths perilous to pass.
Scree slopes slip, undermining any calm.
Edges, cliffs, chasms call gravity vast.
Who will guard, guide my side, keep me
from harm?

Thin air no filter of sun's burning sting.
Dry heat draws moisture 'til thirst becomes pain.
Bright light shines, blinding with glistering bling.
Who will guard, over shade, freshen with rain?

Anxious depression, disorders of mind,
Old lunacies, now better understood,
still draw in horizons, tighten the bind.
Who will guard, shield with care – mind,
soul, heart's good?

Maker of mountains, the mover of stone.
Mountains need crossing, but I'm not alone.

Psalm 122 ~ Worship

We long for a gate; a liminal space
Where our feet rest eased, in sacred enfold
Where our hearts find calm in your hiding place
The house of the Lord an ascent of gold

Where tribes go on up; a holy nation
Where we shout your praise and
then lean; consoled
Where we know pure joy in adoration
Your statutes are good; delight to our souls

So we pray for peace in our weary towns
And long for repose in our restless homes
Fling colours of spring o'er our faithless ground
And sprinkle your balm wherever we roam

You will breathe peace through all of our cages
Write all that's good on all of our pages

PSALM 122 ~ WORSHIP

Pausing at the threshold, a gateway to
A spacious place where gladness and joy flow.
Walking with, not lock step forced two by two,
but woven crowds sharing one way to go.

Following the direction, see and taste,
Thankful hearts sing praise to the Almighty.
Coming to the throne of judgment and grace
to hear the Word that speaks life over me.

In this place plead for the city of peace.
O Jerusalem, God's people's homestead
So torn and divided, Jesus still weeps.
Pray for the deep well-being intended.

We're God's holy temple, one neighbourhood.
I call peace over, in, through you, for good.

PSALM 123 ~ SERVICE

Watch the eyes of the servant waiting for
the sign, nod, wink – attentive, perceptive.
Always looking up, ready to move or
stay, still, reasonable service to give.

The master of mercy's hands wide open,
Grace that gives freely, no limits on love.
We do not deserve, it's just heaven's scent,
as God bends near in embrace from above.

So many chains to ensnare and beguile—
Addicted to work, status, or money.
Weighed down by contempt and words full of bile.
We need help to flee, to truly be free.

Kneeling before us, he washes our feet.
The servant master, our pattern to meet.

Psalm 123 ~ Service

I tune out my mind and look to the heights
Where you sit, divine, far over us all
I kneel away pride as I touch the skies
And leave me behind in my master's call

I wait for respite in holy spring rain
Your mercy a balm to my world-drained soul
No need to earn it; you bend once again
Your favour is wild; extravagance rolls.

Save me from danger, from all that confines
From thorns round my heart, from scorn's
wretched hold
All the vain charms of this earth's lesser shrines
I leave behind to find all things consoled.

All of your grace is my liberation
Mercy is sky-vast; love is salvation.

Psalm 124 ~ Help

I'd be devoured if it wasn't for you,
Shame and despair, sickness and lies
Deceits of this world, impeding my view
Swallowed by fear if you weren't on my side.

I'd be submerged if it wasn't for you
Doubt's waterfalls crashing down on my head
Floods of anxiety lash me anew
Without you near me I'd sink in deep dread

I'd be caged in if it wasn't for you
Fractured wings crumbling, a prey to unease
You smash the world's guile-traps; slice
them all through
You shatter my snares and drench me in peace

My help is in you, oh crafter of worlds
You stay by my side; I soar as a bird

Psalm 124 ~ Help

If the Lord God had not been on our side
Then they would have swallowed us up,
dragged down
to the depths with angry mouths gaping wide.
Deep lurking monsters would have gone to town.

If the Lord God had not been on our side
Then flash flood flows would have washed us away,
to drown in the breaking waves at high tide.
Overwhelming foes would have had their day.

If the Lord God had not been on our side
Then the traps would have sprung, holding us tight
Pursued and harried with nowhere to hide.
Walls closing in would have brought in the night.

But God's with us, for us, ever the same.
By our side, on our side, sing out God's name.

PSALM 125 ~ SECURITY

Solid foundations trust digs in deep rock
of God's mountain strong promise and word.
Settled and rooted, firm braced 'gainst life's knocks,
abiding forever with my true Lord.

Fences of peaks that keep out the forces
ever prowling around. You surround me
Lord, creator of granite stone courses.
You're my soul's shelter, I'll rest in Your lee.

Sovereign protector, portion provider,
earth's government leaders under your sway
can never implement evil so wide
until your people have no righteous way.

Restful reward comes to those who hold fast
Ever choose trust in the first and the last.

PSALM 125 ~ SECURITY

Trusting can hurt when life falls in shadows,
But there's still a mountain that won't be moved
You are secure; you rest on high meadows,
God's word forever the summit of truth

You feel surrounded by pain's aching spaces
But there's still a mountain that won't be moved
You may be broken by fear's wounded places
God's love surrounds you, the Spirit still soothes

You sometimes stumble, and let your eyes fall
But there's still a mountain that won't be moved
Keep your heart blazing, your soul standing tall
God's justice honours, and will not accuse.

Peace be upon you, and peace be your song
Peace be within you and peace be life long

PSALM 126 ~ JOY

Broken buildings repaired, salted fields farmed,
Shop windows once boarded, bright with display.
Children scamper, lovers wander, all's calm,
Where fortune's restored, a sun bright beach day.

Laughter bubbled, joy overflowed, the Lord
brought back home all the lost and the captives.
A reversal resounding, led to more
rejoicing at the greatness of God's gifts.

Holding joy in what's been anchors our prayer
for rain on dry deserts, streams in parched lands,
Grubby streets washed with rivers of your care.
In weeping distress, we reach for pierced hands.

Sowing with faith in the harvest High King
We trust sorrow's seeds will bloom with blessing.

PSALM 126 ~ JOY

When you burst through before, we stood in awe
Floodgates of power a deluge of dreams
We ruptured in laughter, flung wide joy's door
Your marvels our wonder, surging like streams

We dreamed in praise and the nations were dazed
'The Lord's done great things', rung out
through the night
We danced through our days and soaked
in joy's rays
And how our mourning was still our delight

Now we wait in wasteland, yearning for rain
Our tears are our food, our song lost in cloud
You've done it before, you'll do it again
Cascade your flood over this arid ground

Even when hearts go out weary and void
We'll laugh till we cry, returning with joy

PSALM 127 ~ WORK

My heart's a house for God's Holy Spirit.
Wonky walls, leaky roof, whole site's a fright.
Labour I might, alone I can't fix it.
But God's at work with me, building me right.

The church is God's house, living stones roused
in one holy purpose. "Watch" is our call.
We slumber slothful, eyes heavy, drowsy.
But God's at work in us, guarding our walls.

Houses have many shapes, families too:
Blended, extended, chosen, adopting.
Not always easy, much wiping up poo.
But God's at work through them, blessing to bring.

God's love gives rest to those who trusting, stop,
and reposing receive good from our God.

PSALM 127 ~ WORK

In the beginning, you weaved with all might
Your work resplendent through creation's house
Had you not formed it, then dark might
quench light
Vanity's void, if your hand did not plough.

When we strive alone, we gamble our home
Weary and laden by empty work weight
Babel's futility becomes our own
So may we seek you and build up your gates.

When we drift in languor, we drop your call
Inertia's grip cracks our walls and our floors
Family strength drained by lethargy's fall
So may we seek you and build up your doors.

You grant us deep rest, and in such our needs,
In your abundance our work will succeed.

PSALM 128 ~ HAPPINESS

We have enough when we gaze at your face
Lavish joy sparks when we lay ourselves down
Our souls at rest in luxuriant grace
So we will kneel; in delight we will bow.

We have enough when we seek what you give
Free us from excess, from craving for more
Our cups overflow as long as we live
May we share harvests through wide-open doors.

We have enough when we love what we hold
Our homes and our people, gems of great worth
Tables of gladness, adorned sacred gold
So we will praise you for all that you birth.

May we taste blessing like sun-sparkled rays
May we live peace-soaked through all of our days.

PSALM 128 ~ HAPPINESS

Blessing began, Word spoken – light and life.
Content pleasure Creator's intention
Saw garden grown for first husband and wife.
Goodness and glory shot through creation.

Blessing between found by those who don't take:
Spirit poor, mourning, gentle strong, hungry,
mercy shower, pure hearted, peace maker,
picked on. All who walk the way humbly.

Blessing builds on at time's consummation.
A new Jerusalem descends, God dwells,
wiping tears, calming fears of the nations.
Faith's generations no fell hell can quell.

Blessing brings peace to all of God's people
Be happy, enjoy, revel in heart's deep.

PSALM 129 ~ PERSEVERANCE

Besieged not beaten, bullied not broken.
Loud voices surround, pulling me downward.
Still voice inside, repeating words spoken
over, reassure, build up, call homeward.

Stripped and whipped, furrows ploughed
on a field back.
Deep heart hurts dealt by betrayal in torn
trust. Head, hands, feet pierced. Breath robbed
by the rack.
It is done, finished, completed. All's borne.

May hate's harvest fail, wounding words wither,
their planting as thatch straw, barren of grain.
No fruitful fields by malice's river,
All of that effort expended in vain.

Bonds broken, traces cut, God puts things right,
"My yoke is easy and burden is light."

Psalm 129 ~ Perseverance

A life lived in scourges, still castigating
Sickness berating, my fear an old friend
Let me repeat: such trials devastating
But they don't own me; they won't be my end.

I sink to the ground, yet lift up my face,
My body wounded, but you are still here,
They will not triumph; I'll still run this race
When the clouds gather I'll still persevere.

Like untended plants, may they wilt away,
May their power fail; their harvest regress
Sickness won't flourish; and fear will decay
None may declare that these curses are blessed

God, you are righteous, you set my heart free;
You scatter my bonds to faraway seas.

PSALM 130 ~ HOPE

I wander the depths, I search for your light
Soul sore with weeping, I'm seeking relief
Come and dispel my anguish-dark night
Break through the shadows and shatter my grief

If you marked my failures I would not stand
But you don't keep records of all my mess
I'm hidden deep in eternity's hand
I yearn to serve you and soak in your rest

All my wild edges are craving your peace
Waiting in pieces as I long for you
Your words of life bring my soul to its knees
I'll wait through pain till your sweet morning dew

May wide ocean-hope cascade all our days
Borderless love call our unending gaze.

Psalm 130 ~ Hope

Passing through dark depths I call out to God,
"Attend to my plea, Lord, hear my heart's cry.
If you kept track, Lord, of our sinful plod
No one could stand. But you, Lord, show mercy."

Worship responds in reverent service,
As forgiveness flows free, mending the torn.
I scan the horizon for first light's kiss,
The rosy lipped promise of dayspring dawn.

Hocked souls bought back by heaven's great
treasure.
Owing no forfeit, released from all debt.
Perfect redemption – love without measure.
Every accounting by the Word met.

In pain I'll wait, watching, hope I'll confess,
Never forgetting God's faithful fullness.

Psalm 131 ~ Humility

Healthy humility, winsome and kind,
Sees self clearly, delights in achievement,
Mine or another's, no envy in mind.
Not put down, built up – humility's scent.

Proudly ambition lusts to be lifted,
Eyes bigger than bellies seek greener fields.
Pruned to aspiration, all self sifted,
Brings harvest of glory, heavy fruit yields.

Milky lips cry loud, demanding their due.
Babies grow up, not squalling to suckle.
Solid food eating, now able to chew,
Resting still in calm trust that won't buckle.

Now and forever, we'll look to the Lord,
Letting aspiring trust be our soul's ward.

PSALM 131 ~ HUMILITY

The world always crowds us, striving for more
Be better, be greater; we must be proud—
Cling to the truth because discontent's roar
Rages and cages and crushes us loud.

Aching for calm in our wilds of unrest
Turn to the sacred for comfort profound
An infant in arms, all new from the breast
Contentment's relief our confident ground

Leaving dependence, yet leaning on arms
of love eternal, where arrogance melts
Learning to walk, to thrive in life's harms
Contentment a stream where quietness dwells

We wait and we hope; you hear our heart cries
We linger with you where pure love abides.

PSALM 132 ~ OBEDIENCE

Remember me as I think on your deeds
How I yearn for home, to be with you there,
I find you on hills, embrace you in fields
You are my fountain and my very air.

May I create space in my heart and home
To welcome you here; to honour you first
May I yield rest to establish your throne,
Pursue you with passion; deepen my thirst.

You chose to abide here, dwell in our midst,
To shower your love, and clothe us in praise
Shroud us in glory, in holy-flame kiss
And we will shout joy through pain-scented days.

May radiant light anoint us anew,
May we live to kneel; to celebrate you.

Psalm 132 ~ Obedience

Recall David's fervour, vow making lips.
Law tablet ark, mercy seat, manna bed,
God's presence marker, focus of worship.
He brought it home dancing, doing as he said.

God's promised oath, hope's firm foundation laid
Anchors obedience to the true rock.
Covenant commitments keep on the way,
walking trusting with God, safe in the flock.

God will abide, reside, rest in the midst,
more than bless, fill food banks, overflowing
joy will spill jubilant shouts from faith kissed
hearts. Love's light more gloriously glowing.

Lamp lit, shining crown of splendour prepared
For David's heir, chrismed High King fore'er.

PSALM 133 ~ COMMUNITY

Oil's flow, aromatic blended fragrance,
glistens, lubricates, smooths away frictions.
Spirit sign, worship pours out, God's servants
anointed whole, no distillate fractions.

Beard's flow, rich, mature, abundant glories.
Every body priestly robed, royal,
chosen, holy, together tell stories
of God whose marv'lous light shines like shook foil.

Dew's flow, morning refreshment falls sweetly,
revival for parched lands, new life green shoots.
Hearts dry and lonely, hydrated gently,
find friendship's flourish, restoring deep roots.

Life's good and pleasant in community.
Brothers, sisters, God blesses unity.

PSALM 133 ~ COMMUNITY

The wonder of joyful community
Blazes of colour across ev'ry land
When God's people ally in unity
Through all our struggles – united we stand.

Copious warmth in extravagant oil,
Cascading down in abundant display
A river bursts banks and floods thirsty soil,
How satisfying is kinship's array.

Foothills of Hermon, rejoice and be slaked,
Dewdrop-drenched wastelands, now
surging with life,
Poverty perish and plenty awake,
Unity's profit sets us on new heights.

Eternity's artist painting new skies,
As life is restored, as one we will rise.

Psalm 134 ~ Blessing

Lift up your eyes when night wraps murky dark,
When dusk coils its tendrils, raise up your gaze,
Kneel through your gloom-hours, and seek
out joy's spark—
Touch sacred summits in unceasing praise.

Lift up your hands when wounds wrap sore around,
When agony shivers, soar through jewelled skies
of upside-down mercy; grace that abounds—
Drenched in soul-freedom, abide in love's prize.

Lift up your soul when life wraps luring snares,
When world-flavour dazzles, rise on praise-wings
Find holy spaces, where incense-swelled air
weaves and entwines you, and winter is spring.

Creator of colour, firer of stars,
Oh God of the broken, tend to our scars.

PSALM 134 ~ BLESSING

You are invited, beckoned, welcomed in,
"Bless the Lord." Leave your fear,
shame, foolishness.
Forgiven all, washed clean, set free to sing,
Chorus worship wonder with joyfulness.

You're commanded, directed, instructed,
"Bless the Lord." Lift your hands, though
feelings fail.
In the dawnless dark, on your sleepless bed,
Choose life, remember grace, praises exhale.

A crescendo – speaking well, calling good,
Falling favour, spirals, builds up, weaves round.
Blessings flow, overspilling, as they should.
Blessed to be a blessing, God's people found.

May the Lord, maker of heaven above
and earth beneath, bless you with God's great love.

Books by Tim and Liz Carter

Tim:
Being Sent: Jonah's mission, Our Mission, God's Mission

Liz:
Catching Contentment: How to be Holy Satisfied
Treasure in Dark Places: Stories and poems of hope in the hurting
Valuable: Why your worth is not defined by how useful you feel
Coming in Winter 2023: *Repression Ground: #1 in the Newland Trilogy – a dystopian thriller*

Find us at:

www.greatadventure.carterclan.me.uk
www.carterclan.me.uk/sermons

Printed in Great Britain
by Amazon

24886784R00030